Super Lexi
Is Not a Fan of Christmas

SUPER LEXI

Is Not a Fan of Christmas

by Emma Lesko

Illustrated by
Adam Winsor

Red Leather Books, LLC

Text copyright © 2014 by Emma Lesko
Illustrations copyright © 2014 by Adam Winsor
Interior design by Typeflow

First paperback edition in this format 2014

ISBN 978-0-9914310-1-4 (paperback)

The illustrations were painted in Photoshop.

Red Leather Books, LLC.
2713 Salk Avenue, Suite 250
Carlsbad, CA 92008

Learn more about Super Lexi at
www.EmmaLesko.com

Contents

1

Hoopla

I knew I was doomed at indoor recess today when Ruhan sang, "Walkin' 'round in purple underwear." That's actually part of a song about Christmas lights and snow. Only, Ruhan likes to mess up the words. When people sing Christmas music, hoopla is breathing down my neck.

Hoopla is a big, fat party. It's practically a college word. I know all about it even though I'm only in second grade. It's loud like an explosion. Also, it's full of surprises. I have a phobia of those things. They make my insides hard like an ice cube. Also, they make my mouth slam shut and trap words in there. Plus, they give me a feeling of barf.

Most of the kids in my class like parties. That's okay, though. Everybody's different from everybody, and I'm different about hoopla.

I tried to shut my ears from Ruhan. I needed my brains to think about other stuff. My best friend, Kaylee, and I were making a paper fortune-teller at desk fifteen. All kids have superpowers. One of mine is folding paper like an expert. One of Kaylee's is tiny writing. That's how come we're the perfect fortune-teller team.

"Can you write a fortune that says, 'You

will not have Christmas hoopla?'" I asked.

"Sure!" she said.

Some parts of Kaylee are like me. For example, she only wears boys' clothes and does not like pink. Some parts of her are not like me, though. For example, Christmas hoopla is her favorite.

"Maybe you better add, 'If your name is not Kaylee,'" I said. I didn't want to screw up her future.

The bell rang, and I jumped. I am a very jumpy person. The bell means bottoms-in-seats because recess is done.

So bad news.

Kaylee didn't have time to write that fortune.

We put our gel pens back in the box. Christopher crawled around looking for board game pieces. Isa and Phoebe squealed because he farted on purpose.

Bottoms-in-seats is never quiet.

My ears are not fans of that. They are very strong ears. Practically supersonic.

That's how come I had to pretend it was time for the only part of school I love love love. Silent reading. When I read, it's the only time I'm an expert at tuning out.

I got my new book from the library out of my desk. It's about a bunny family. They eat yummy food and read books. They live in a cave under the ground for the whole winter. Even though I'm human, I'm like a bunny. I would like Christmas to be quiet in a cozy cave.

My book was so good that I missed my teacher's important announcement. Her name is Joan, but only if you're a grown-up. If you're a kid, it's Ms. Kleinert.

"Lexi, did you hear me?" she asked. She was standing by the big calendar on the bulletin board.

"Yes," I said.

"Can you answer the question?"

"I heard your voice. Not your words," I said.

"Please put your book away, Lexi. Who can tell me what a Present Partner is?"

I felt confused about that.

Lots of kids raised their hands. Phoebe's was the highest. She's a princess girl who wears sparkly stuff on her face. "It's when we pick a name from a hat. Then we give a present to that person," she said.

"That's correct, Phoebe," said Ms. Kleinert. "Next Friday, we'll have a Present Partner Party!" She pointed at that day on the calendar. Lots of the days were already filled up with paper dreidels and ornaments. I did not have the courage to count how many empty squares were left.

That party sounded like hoopla. I had a feeling it was going to have cookies and catchy tunes and blabby kids with too much sugar in them. Then my eardrums would explode. Plus, I would get the feeling of barf.

All the kids squealed and wiggled. Except for me. I felt hot. Christopher wiggled most of all. He sits in desk thirteen and I'm in desk fourteen even though I never actually agreed to that. Christopher gets very inside my personal space. Also, he chases me with snots.

I put my arms around my stomach and groaned. The heater blew hot air on me. The snowflakes we made in art floated around on their ceiling strings. I got dizzy staring at those.

I raised my hand. "Yes, Lexi?" asked Ms. Kleinert.

"It's just that I don't know when you were planning on doing this," I said. "On account of on Fridays we have journals. Then math facts. Then language—"

"Next Friday will be a little different," said Ms. Kleinert. "So, we'll have to remember to go with the flow."

"Lexi never goes with the flow!" yelled Christopher, the blurtface.

I slumped in my chair.

Ms. Kleinert moved his clip to the big, fat trouble clipboard. "Now," she said. "You're going to write your names on these little pieces of paper. Then, put them in this ski hat. Take one and pass it down."

I followed that rule. Only, then I got confused about how this was going to work.

I raised my hand again.

"Yes, Lexi?" said Ms. Kleinert.

"It's just that I won't know who to give my Christmas list to," I said.

"No lists, Lexi. Each Present Partner will choose their gifts."

"Yes, but I am not a fan of surprises," I said. The only present on my whole list is a plastic snowman. He spits out candy when you press his belly. It's my favorite toy on Planet Earth.

"We get what we get, and we don't throw a fit," said Ms. Kleinert.

She always says that when she means business.

I was doomed.

Everybody got chatty except for me. I got terrified. My eardrums were already blaring. My insides turned into cement.

Christopher leaned over and said, "I

already know what I'm going to get my Present Partner." I didn't know if he was trying to scare me or what. He was probably going to buy an ant farm or something. I could already feel ants crawling on my legs.

I needed a plan. I thought very hard for a while. My brains were frozen solid. Then an idea popped in. Everything melted back to normal. I was going to pick my own name. I'd buy my own present. Then I'd have one less thing to worry about at that hoopla party.

After I wrote my name, I folded the paper into the shape of a teensy bird. That's how I'd know it was mine. When Ms. Kleinert came by, I dropped it in the ski hat.

A few minutes later, she shook up the hat. She walked around the room. When Christopher's turn came, I got a flutter in my belly. My turn was next. I was excited about buying myself that snowman.

My turn came. I felt around for the tiny bird. I didn't feel it.

"Take one quickly, Lexi, we have a lot to pass out," said Ms. Kleinert.

I dug around. There were only papers with normal folds. Then Christopher said, "Oh, great. I got Lexi." That's Christmas for you. Nothing ends up the way you expect.

I picked a paper and didn't even look at it.

My body slid down my chair until my head was on the seat. I was certain my bottom landed on a pokey staple and that it was bleeding to death. Ms. Kleinert did not notice. She was busy making kids pick names. That made them very blabby and loud.

My bottom sat on the pokey staple for a long time. I saw a chewed-up piece of gum under my desk. It gave me the feeling of barf.

Gum on furniture is very against the rules. I gave that lump a terrible, angry face. The party wasn't even here yet and I was already a big grump.

I looked out the window and wished for

the day to end. Giant snowflakes fell all over the place out there. They looked peaceful. I wanted to feel peaceful. I stared at those beautiful flakes until they blurred.

The only good thing was that Kaylee leaned over to me. She whispered, "Don't worry, Lexi. It'll be OK."

For a second I felt better. Then I remembered she always says that, and it never is.

2

The Excellent Paper Chain

After school, I had a plan to fix my bad day. "I'm going to watch violent cartoons and eat junk food," I said to my mom. She was pushing the couches around the TV room. That was not thoughtful. The TV room is supposed to look the same always. It's where people go to relax.

"No TV today, Lexi. We have a busy afternoon. I'm going to need your help."

"I never actually agreed to that," I said.

"Remember we talked about it this morning?"

"No," I said. I slumped. That's what I do when I compromise. A compromise is when you agree to do something you don't actually like. Then, I tried to scoot the couch back

to the right spot. It did not budge.

"I'd rather you do spec check than move that."

"Spec check" is the mom word for "Crawl around the floor and pick up stuff." So, bad news, I had to do that.

I grabbed an old sock from under the couch. The carpet smelled like milk down there. Plus, it was not squished and flat like in the rest of the room. "I'm not sure why we're doing this," I said. I pulled out a crumpled juice box. "It's not going to be easy watching violent cartoons from a couch that's in the wrong place."

"We're making room for the Christmas tree," she said.

That's when I got horrified. Christmas tree shopping means getting carsick because it's far away. It means you have to stand in the cold until your toes freeze solid, too. Also, it means you have to get sad that all those trees don't have roots anymore.

I tried not to think about that. I picked popcorn bits out of the carpet.

"I'm going to grab the Christmas boxes from the basement," said Mom. "Do you want to come down with me?"

"Don't go! You'll catch on fire," I said.

"Lexi, for the hundredth time, the basement is not going to catch on fire."

"Well, I saw flames in a crack in the furnace, so . . ."

"It's safe, Lexi. It's how a furnace works," she said.

I took my spec check junk to the garbage can. "Good luck," I said.

After she went downstairs, I plopped down in front of my guinea pig Fred's cage. I'm lucky. I can do crisscross applesauce anywhere because I don't wear skirts. That's sitting with your legs like a pretzel. Too bad the tile floor was cold. Creepy basement air leaked everywhere. I wished my mom could keep the scary door shut.

I forgot about all that fast, though, because Fred got happy to see me. He poked his nose through his cage wires. He is an excellent friend. Also, he smells like wood chips, which makes me feel very cuddly.

I petted his head with my finger. It's soft, like dandelion fuzz. I picked him out of all the guinea pigs at the pet store because his hair is messy like mine.

"I have a big problem," I said.

Fred squeaked.

"Christmas got even worse today."

I took the tiny piece of paper out of my

pocket. "Someone's name is on this. I'm supposed to buy this kid a present. Only I can't because I have a phobia of that party. I can't even look at it," I said. I thought about letting him eat it. That would be an awful thing to do, though. I kept that tiny paper inside my fist.

"I wish I counted the empty squares on the calendar at school today. I don't even remember what day today is," I said.

Fred looked at me. He wanted answers.

"I guess I could count how many loops are left on the crummy chain I had to make," I said. I made that thing out of red and green paper in art class. I thought it was a count-down to winter break. Now I knew it was also a countdown to the Present Partner Party.

My mom hung it up by the junk food cup-board. Every day, I have to rip off a loop.

When there are no more loops left, guess what. Hoopla.

"It's too bad I had to use my chain skills for such a crummy thing." I said. "It's actually quite excellent." I went over to it. I ripped a loop off that chain. I counted the ones that were left. The answer was not pleasant.

"It's worse than I thought." My voice was a teensy squawk. That happens when bad surprises come and slam my mouth shut. Only nine loops.

I shoved the loop in Fred's cage. He thinks paper is yummy. He gobbled it up. Then, he looked at me. He wanted more. That's how I got a super idea. I went to the craft box in the closet. I got paper, scissors, and glue. Then I ran to the basement door. I could hear my mom pushing heavy boxes around. They made scraping noises on the cement floor.

I felt worried about her down there. "Any fire?" I asked.

"No, Lexi."

"When are you coming up?" I asked.

"Ten minutes! You need something?"

"Perfect," I said to Fred.

I made sixteen more loops. Two for Fred, fourteen for the countdown chain. I cut things very well. I practiced scissor skills a lot in kindergarten. Now I cut like a grown-up. "Actually, this makes me feel quite peaceful," I said to Fred.

He nibbled on his paper. That was a cute thing to see. It disappeared into his tiny mouth very fast. "I think you're cheering me up," I said. He picked up the next loop with his mouth. It looked like a big tongue. He did a happy squeal and jump just for me.

"You are an excellent friend," I said. The

rest of the chain-making was the best part of my day. I even found a place to hide the tiny paper I took out of that ski hat at school. I taped it right under Fred's food bowl. I did not even peek at the kid's name on that thing. "Now I don't have to think about that for a while."

When it was all done, I felt relief. "Phew!" I said. "I think I bought us some time."

3

Rattling Chain Saw Teeth

Breaking news. I did not buy us some time. My mom didn't fall for the Christmas chain trick for one tiny second. Next thing I knew, I was sitting in a wagon at the tree farm. My dad was pulling me. It was cozy, though. The whole place looked covered in marshmallow fluff. Also, the moon made everything sparkle. I snuggled in fuzzy blankets so I didn't even feel frozen stiff. They smelled like the dryer.

We followed a guy with big earflaps on his hat. He was taking us to his favorite spot where the good trees were supposed to be. Even though it was dark out, I could see he was carrying a huge chain saw with sharp teeth. They rattled.

I tried not to think about that scary thing because I had very good news to celebrate: Kaylee was with us.

Kaylee didn't sit in the wagon. "I'm going to drag my feet in the snow so people think someone skied here," she said. Her feet made a scrape-scrape noise.

"Actually, that is a very good job," I said.

"It's how you get around at the North Pole," she said.

"This looks like the North Pole," said Daddy. "Especially there." He pointed to Santa's Workshop. It was lit up with Christmas lights. People waited in a giant line that went all the way to the parking lot.

"It looks like a gingerbread house!" said Kaylee.

"I bet that chimney's not made with real gumdrops," I said. "They're probably wood or something."

"Lexi, use your imagination," she said.

"I don't have one," I said, on account of that's true. "That candy cane fence is fake, too."

"Well, you're destroying the magic a little," said Kaylee.

"Oops. I didn't actually know that," I said. I shut my trap. I got traumatized at Santa's Workshop last year. I got smooshed by lots of people in line. Also, it smelled like wet socks. I didn't tell Kaylee that, though. I am not a fan of destroying her magic.

"Can we see Santa after?" she asked.

"Sure!" said Mom. "Lexi, I need some new garland for the tree. Would you like to come with me to the Christmas shop? Or would you like to go see Santa with Dad and Kaylee?"

Kaylee closed her eyes and asked, "Please, please, please?" The top of her hair had moonlight all over it.

"Door two," I said.

"Yay!" yelled Kaylee. She did her smile that shows all her missing teeth.

That reminded me of chain saw teeth. I peeked over at them while Kaylee cheered. I did a secret little shiver.

I decided to look at the Christmas trees instead of that terrifying thing. We were walking toward a forest now. I sniffed a big, cold sniff. "All that extra oxygen smells like pine needles and campfires," I said.

"I can see your oxygen when you talk!" said Kaylee.

My breath was a white poof in the air. Only, it was actually my carbon dioxide. I read about that in my almanac. I didn't say that out loud on account of Kaylee's feelings. Instead, I said, "The trees breathe our breath, and we breathe theirs. That's how come they're such good friends."

Kaylee made her mouth into a big O. "Am I making rings?" she asked. Only, she wasn't.

"You look horrified," I said, and Mom, Daddy, and Kaylee laughed.

Then Daddy put his mouth in a crooked shape and said, "Am I making Z's?"

That guy is hilarious. We all laughed white puffs into the air.

"I wonder what our puffs would look like if we had hot chocolate," I said.

"We'll have to get some and experiment," said Daddy.

Kaylee and I both did a cheer then. That's how I forgot all about those chain saw teeth for good. "Breaking news!" I said. "This errand is actually spectacular."

"What do you say we grab a tree here and get that hot chocolate?" said Mom.

I lay down in the wagon while the grown-ups and Kaylee inspected trees for bare spots. The stars were twinkly, and the moon was gigantic. Only a few people walked around with crunching wagon wheels like us. I put the blanket over my face. My carbon dioxide felt warm. I thought about hot chocolate with marshmallows. My insides were as calm as giant snowflakes.

That's how come I wasn't ready for the explosion in my eardrums.

The loudest noise on Planet Earth blared. All of my insides felt hot and spikey at the same time. I tried to run, but everything got hard like an ice cube.

I saw a big, black shadow of Mr. Earflaps. He held up the chain saw in the moonlight.

He looked like a scary Halloween guy.

It's possible that I screamed very loud.

Mr. Earflaps sliced a tall tree with his evil chain saw. When I get super-strong feelings, I want words to burst out. Only, they get stuck inside my brains. I tried to yell, "You're hurting it!" Too bad I couldn't. The tree leaned over slowly. It looked very sad. Finally, it fell onto the snow, and the chain saw turned off.

I was furious at everybody.

I yelled in my brains, *It makes oxygen, you know!* I'm very grateful to trees for that favor. I was not a fan of that earflap guy for killing it. I wished I could blurt that out.

Daddy picked me up. My body could not cuddle. Kaylee patted my back. Mom held my hand. Mr. Earflaps threw the poor tree on my wagon. It slumped like it was making a compromise. Everyone walked back, very silent because of the terrible thing that happened. The tree branches bounced from the bumps in the road.

When we got back to the parking lot, Mr. Earflaps tied the tree to the roof of the car. It looked skinny and sad up there.

Daddy was still holding me. I was very stiff. "How about that hot cocoa, Lexi?" he asked.

"No!" I said.

I gave Mr. Earflaps the angriest, meanest look my face parts could make.

"If you don't act good, you'll get on the

naughty list," he said. "Then you don't get to celebrate Christmas."

"We'll handle it, thank you," said Mom.

"Why don't Lexi and I wait in the car, while you take Kaylee to see Santa," my dad said to her.

"I want to stay with Lexi," said Kaylee.

So guess what. No garland for my mom. No Santa for Kaylee. No hot cocoa with marshmallows for anyone. I felt a teensy bit awful about that.

Just about the only good thing was that the earflap guy gave me an idea.

4

The Top-Secret Plan

"I want to go see Santa today," I said at breakfast. I had a top-secret plan to get out of the Present Partner Party. I was going to get on the naughty list.

Our house smelled like eggnog French toast and bacon. I got to eat that at a TV table in the living room because it was Saturday. I was watching cartoons while Daddy scrubbed pots and pans in the kitchen. I was starting to like the new spot for the couch because it was right by the heating vent now. My feet felt toasty.

Mom stuck our Christmas tree in a big bowl on the floor so it could drink water and make us oxygen. She grunted a lot while she wiggled it in there. "Are you sure you want to see Santa, Lexi?" she asked. "You haven't enjoyed that in the past."

"Maybe we could find a Santa who doesn't have many fans," I said. "Like the one who stands by the drugstore."

I made a wish that my parents would say "yes." I crossed my fingers, only that can't make a wish come true by itself. So, I crossed my toes and eyeballs, too.

"Sounds like a great idea," yelled Daddy from the sink.

"Hooray!" I said. Things were looking up.

"Can we invite Kaylee?"

"That's thoughtful," said Mom. She screwed screws real tight in the water bowl. Then she walked over to me. She scrunched down to talk at me. Her head blocked my cartoons. "It sounds like you feel guilty because Kaylee didn't get to see Santa last night. She doesn't blame you, Lexi."

I licked powdered sugar off a piece of French toast. "Duh. I didn't chain saw an innocent thing," I said. "But I can still help undestroy her magic."

After breakfast, we drove to the drugstore on Main Street. They let you walk around in bare feet during summer there. Kaylee and I had boots, though. It was a North Pole kind of day. Snow fell in giant globs. The only cars we saw the whole way there were a salt truck and a snowplow.

Santa stood outside ringing a bell. The drugstore looked a little like his workshop, all covered up in snow behind him. Christmas lights twinkled in the windows. There was almost no noise. Snow makes the outside sound very silent.

"It's actually my favorite kind of day," I said.

"Mine too!" said Kaylee. She stuck out her tongue and ate snowflakes.

My belly did a little flop. I could tell it was the kind of day when good luck happened.

"Do you want to talk to Santa before or after we go in the store, girls?" asked Daddy.

"After!" said Kaylee. "I might want to add stuff to my list."

"Door two," I said. I wanted to tell Kaylee all about my top-secret plan.

Inside felt like a cozy bunny cave. We were

the only shoppers on account of Daddy said not everybody is adventurous like us. I liked how quiet it was. The best part was that the middle aisle wasn't filled with rakes and patio furniture like usual. Instead, it over-flowed with candy and toys and big blow-up decorations. Kaylee and I got to go there by ourselves because of the buddy system. It smelled like gummy bears.

"This is a spectacular aisle," I said.

"It's a Christmas miracle!" said Kaylee. "I want everything." She picked up lots of stuff with her purple mittens. Also, she pressed buttons on the toys that played Christmas music. I watched my parents to make sure they went very far away. When I couldn't hear their voices, it was time to tell Kaylee the news.

She was wearing furry red earmuffs instead

of a hat. She likes her poofy pigtails to show. I lifted an earmuff away from her ear, and I whispered, "I have to get on Santa's naughty list."

"Why?" she asked.

"It's the only way out of the Present Partner Party."

She knows all about how my hoopla phobia. Good friends know that stuff. She looked right at my face. "You don't really break rules, Lexi. You don't break promises, and you never lie. Plus, you never cheat. You don't even say mean things to hurt feelings. That's why you're my best friend."

"I have to pretend," I said.

"OK," she said.

I am a fan of the way Kaylee always says "OK." She doesn't say stuff like "Everybody likes Christmas hoopla, Lexi!" like other people.

Kaylee started picking up candy and looking at it again. A red lightbulb reindeer nose blinked on the shelf by her head. "So are you going to steal the money out of Santa's bucket or something?"

"That's a good idea," I said.

"Are you going to cut off his beard?"

"I didn't think of that."

"You could put dog poop right where he's going to walk!"

She was very good at this.

"Or I could throw a snowball at his face," I said.

She covered her mouth with her mitten. "Man, you'll get on the naughty list for sure."

Inside I secretly hoped I could make Santa think I was naughty without actually breaking rules. "Yep," I said. My voice was teensy.

We got quiet for a few minutes. Kaylee

added lots of junk food to her Christmas list. I looked at the floor. After a while, she said, "Lexi, look! A barfing snowman!"

She was holding my dream present.

My tummy felt like I swallowed a lump of coal. "Do you think I'll get any presents if I get on the naughty list?"

"Maybe from your parents," said Kaylee.

I breathed a big, fat relief breath. "That's true," I said.

"I sure wish there was another way to solve your problem," said Kaylee.

"It's a good solution, actually," I said.

That's how come I got my courage while Daddy paid for stuff at the cash register. It was time.

Outside, snowflakes stuck all over Kaylee's pigtail fluffs and made them even more beautiful.

My cheeks got freezing cold, but my insides felt sweaty. I guess that's what nervous feels like in a blizzard. Mom put dollar bills in our mittens so we could stick them in Santa's red bucket. "Are you sure you girls want to do this alone?" she asked.

"Yep," I said.

Mom and Daddy walked over to the fountain. It had no water in it, but lots of pennies. Kaylee and I went up to Santa. The only noise was from his ringing bell and the snow crunching under our boots. Also, I could hear my heart thumps.

Santa had to help us stick our dollar in his bucket on account of mittens are not graceful.

"Well, thank you, and merry Christmas!" he said. Steam blew out of his mouth when he said that.

"Thanks," said Kaylee. I didn't say a peep.

I didn't want Santa to know I had good manners.

"You're brave girls, coming out in the snow like this!" he said.

I did not know how to answer that.

"You should probably run along to your parents. They look cold." He touched our noses with his gloves and winked.

I wanted to walk away because those were his directions. Only I couldn't. I had to look naughty.

"We won't budge," I said.

"We have to talk to you," said Kaylee.

"Ho ho ho! Sure!" said Santa.

Kaylee went first. She blabbed for a long time. She asked about Mrs. Claus and elves. She asked for a giant, furry fake spider. "That's my number one wish on my whole list," she said. "I'm not scared of bugs." Then she asked for fort stuff, a zombie game, and a bunch of other stuff. She did not ask for a barfy snowman. That was thoughtful.

"That's a mighty fine list! I'll do my best," said Santa. Then he looked at me. "And what would you like for Christmas?"

I got silent on account of nerves. I looked at his boots. They were brown with black flaps covering them. I thought about them stomping around my house while I slept. Even though I don't like strangers in my house, I got sad his boots wouldn't stomp there this year.

I took a big breath like I'm supposed to when I'm not calm. "Do you peek when I need privacy?" I finally asked.

"Ho ho ho! I never peek!" he said.

"Well, I heard the song about you seeing everything, so . . ."

He laughed and rubbed his bowl full of jelly belly. "Your privacy is important. I would never invade it."

This was my only chance.

"Well," I said. "I'm actually an awful child in private."

"Ho ho ho! Nonsense!" he said.

A giant salt truck drove by. It sounded a little like a chain saw. My forehead felt prickly. "You don't know on account of you respect my privacy," I said.

"It's true!" said Kaylee. "She was terrible this year. She threw eggs at babies from her bathroom window! Plus, she punched her grandma in the face!" Kaylee made a punch with her mitten when she said that fat lie.

I felt thankful to Kaylee about that favor. I tried to think of even naughtier things. "I put plastic wrap under the toilet seat. It made a giant mess. Plus, I let the bathtub overflow on purpose," I said.

"Is that so?" asked Santa. He didn't even sound mad.

"Yes. Also, I cut all the towels up into confetti. Only you didn't see that on account of I was in the bathroom."

"I don't see everything. But I *know*."

I started to get the feeling that Santa was not going to fall for this. That's how come my voice got depressed when I said the worst lie left in my head. "I also wrote bad words all over the walls with shaving cream," I said.

He bent over and smiled under the top part of his beard. "Don't you worry. You're going to have lots of presents under your tree on Christmas morning."

I was afraid he'd say that.

5

Breaking Rules
Equals Barf

When there were only five loops on my chain, I got desperate. Five loops meant five days until the Present Partner Party. I had no choice. The only way to get on that naughty list was to actually be naughty.

Only one problem. Breaking rules gives me the feeling of barf.

These are the rules I broke:

1. I brushed my teeth for one min-ute and fifty-six seconds instead of two minutes.
2. I put on a short-sleeved shirt even though it was snowing.
3. I wore socks that did not match.

Too bad nobody even noticed I did those naughty things.

When four loops were left, I tried to do something worse. I hid my daddy's cross-word pen in the snow for twenty minutes. At three loops, I poured shampoo in the toilet then flushed it. At two loops, I did something awful. I wrote swear words in my journal. I did all those very terrible things and did not get in trouble once. All I got was a big, fat tummy ache.

Plus, I could not stop thinking about the

poor kid's name under Fred's bowl. I wished I could at least buy that kid a present. Only, that would not be naughty.

By the time there was only one loop left, I could hardly take the pressure anymore. At lunch that day, I wanted to eat my protein before my dessert more than anything. Only I knew what I had to do. I took a bite of my cookie first. Instead of that bite melting in my mouth, it grew and grew and grew. Also, it was dry and lumpy. Guilt ruins delicious food.

"Are you sick?" asked Kaylee.

Ever since Kaylee and I became friends, we sit together at the fourth grade lunch table, even though we're in second grade. That table is empty at our lunchtime. We have special permission to sit there on account of I am not a fan of getting squished. Besides, lots of food smells bad. My nose is as strong as my ears. It's practically a superpower. So I need my distance.

Kaylee's superpower is knowing exactly how I feel without making me tell her.

I put my head down. She patted it. The table felt sticky on my cheek.

"The naughty list?" she asked.

"Yep."

We got quiet for a long time. She tried combing my hair with her fingers. Only, they got stuck. My hair is long on account of scissors are not for me. Mostly, it's knots because brushes are also not for me.

The lights buzzed extra loud that day. They made my head feel pressure. Also, the second grade table was noisy. Christopher was stealing tater tots from the kids who had hot lunch. There was lots of yelling over there.

Finally, Kaylee said, "Why don't you just tell your parents so they can let you skip the party?"

"It's typed on the school calendar!" I said. "It's an official, giant holiday."

She sat there for a while and thought. Her legs were swinging back and forth. I guess that makes solutions come into her head. My seat jiggled because it was attached to hers. I didn't ask her to quit it, though. I needed a good idea to pop into her brains. Eventually, her legs stopped. "Well, tomorrow's the party," she said. "You better skip your sandwich and eat the rest of that cookie."

Bad news, that cookie was rude once it got into my stomach. It hurt me. I think it even swelled up in there. Indoor recess did not help. My classroom always smells like ketchup and milk after that. My naughty list problem was stuck in my brains when Ms. Kleinert had a very serious talk with us.

"Class, some of us are having trouble getting our work done this week," she said. "We're all very excited, but our schoolwork is important."

I did not have trouble getting my work done. I finished my Favorite Winter Memory book. Also, I did my math packet. I showed my work on every page. Also, I didn't have any blanks left in my RCP. That is a reading comprehension packet for a whole entire month. All those things were in a neat stack in my desk.

I was not going to turn that stuff in, though.

It was my last chance for the naughty list.

Ms. Kleinert wrote a list of all our work on the chalkboard. We were supposed to erase our own name when we finished. Then we'd do a quiet choice. "We need to get all this in before the bell rings. Or, I'm afraid we won't be able to have our winter party tomorrow."

The whole class groaned. Except for me. I got a flutter in my belly. I hoped a kid in my class would goof that up. Then I could stop being naughty.

The good news is that everybody got silent for a very long time. They were working hard. I almost felt cozy. The bad news is, by 2:45, everybody started turning stuff in. I read my bunny book and peeked up every now and then. Those names were erasing fast.

Every time a kid erased a name, the quiet choice kids did high fives and quiet cheers. Even Kaylee got excited about the suspense. By 3:00, there was only one name left.

Mine.

Ms. Kleinert said, "Lexi, please turn in

your work."

All the eyeballs in the room stared at me. I have a phobia of that. I tried to say I wasn't turning it in. Instead, my mouth slammed shut.

Without even raising his hand, Christopher said, "Come on, Lexi! I got you the best present ever!" His spit got on my desk. I could feel ants climbing on my legs again.

Phoebe said, "I got sparkly nail polish for my Present Partner."

Ruhan said, "I got slime!"

I felt awful because I didn't get anybody anything.

In half a second, the whole class was yelling stuff at me. My insides got hard. I tried to slide under my desk, but my body would not move. It felt like ants were nibbling me. Ms. Kleinert took a handful of marbles out of the jar. A jar full of marbles equals gum-chewing day. Now we were a whole handful behind because of me. Everybody shut their traps.

"I assume you're working on a quiet choice,

Lexi, because you finished your work?" asked Ms. Kleinert. She is actually a very smart person.

I looked at everybody's eyeballs. I felt the

ants in my hair. The kids waited for me to make a good choice. I was naughtier than I ever thought I could be. It felt terrible. "It's just that I'm not turning them in," I said.

Phoebe yelled, "Don't ruin it for us, Lexi!"

All of a sudden, the bell rang. Everybody scrambled.

I didn't, though. I slumped in my chair. My eyeballs blurred up. The naughty list is a lonely place. It's the worst compromise I ever made.

Ms. Kleinert said, "Lexi, I trust you'll make the right choice. Class, I'll see you tomorrow."

Kaylee looked at me. Her face did not have that smile that shows all her missing teeth. Then she walked out.

So that was that. Because of me, the party was cancelled, I guess.

6

The Worst Feeling
on Planet Earth

The biggest problem with getting on the naughty list is that it can get out of control. Sometimes it can get parties cancelled for a whole class instead of just one kid. That can give a kid guilt.

Guilt is the worst feeling on Planet Earth. It's when all of your insides feel like electricity. Also, your forehead feels like spiders are crawling on it. Also, sweat and goose bumps take turns spreading all over your skin. All those things happened to me when I was in bed that night.

I lay very still like an ice cube the whole time the hall light stayed on under my door. I had a spoon under my pillow. That's supposed to make snow days happen. Then school could get cancelled. Only, the spoon poked me. It did not feel like a lucky thing. Also, my pajamas were on inside out. That's supposed to make snow days happen, too. They did not feel right.

Guilt plus all that stuff equals blech.

I kept telling my brain to shut its trap, but it didn't. It yapped and yapped. It said my parents were not going to be fans of me because I broke all those rules. It called me a bad kid. It told me I ruined Christmas for everybody in my class. Plus, it told me I was breaking the rules again because I was not asleep.

I faked sleep when my parents came in to kiss my forehead. I felt like an awful kid doing that lie. I still had to keep being naughty, though. When the hall light under the door turned off, my body filled with lonely feelings.

I heard whispers. I heard the toilet flush. I heard the bathroom faucet. Then I heard one of my parents flip their light switch. That meant it was dark in the whole entire house. I wished I could turn on the light in my room, but that idea terrified me. I screamed on the inside. Not on the outside, though. On the outside, my voice was tiny. It only said, "Daddy . . . ? Daddy?"

It said that eleven times. Each time, it got a little louder.

All of a sudden, my door opened slowly. My daddy whispered, "Lexi, are you up?" He looked like a big shadow in the dark.

I held my blankets tight next to my face. I nodded my head.

He turned on my dresser lamp, which is not the kind that makes eyes hurt. It made my room look cozy. Daddy sat on my bed and rubbed my hair. He was wearing his squishy blue robe. He smelled like mouthwash. He had bare feet on account of that guy needs a pair of slippers. "What's wrong, kiddo?"

I didn't answer that question.

"Whatever it is, we can find a solution," he said.

Only we couldn't. That's how come I couldn't keep my secrets in me any longer. The next thing I knew, tears fell all over the place.

I told him that I didn't brush my teeth long enough and that I didn't eat my protein first and that I wore socks that didn't match. Then I told him the worst, biggest secret of all. I did not turn in my seatwork. The class party was cancelled.

He looked at me quite serious. This was an important conversation. Half his face was a shadow. "You sound like you regret that," he said.

My voice was a teensy squeak. "Yep," I said.

"Why do you suppose you made those choices?"

"Because I should be on the naughty list," I said. I tried to tell him about the party, but my mouth stopped working.

"All people make bad choices, Lexi. It doesn't make us bad people. What part feels the worst?"

That I ruined the holiday for everybody, I said inside my head. *And now Kaylee's not smiley.*

My cheeks felt itchy and hot. I wiped my face with my sheet. That thing is soft and absorbent. Daddy scratched my head for a while because sometimes that makes me feel better. Only, it didn't.

My nose made lots of noise. So did the furnace.

After a while, Daddy said, "It looks like you're having trouble finding words."

I stared at my wall.

"I'll be right back," he said.

I snuggled up on my pillow. I watched my curtains blow around from the heater. The string from my blinds hit the wall twenty-seven times before Daddy came back. He had a notebook and two gel pens. One sparkly orange and one purple. I thought those were cheerful colors.

"Let's write some possible solutions," he said.

I slumped.

He put the notebook on my pillow. I borrowed the orange pen and wrote: Nothing.

"Hmmm," he said. He tapped his pen on his chin. "How about this." In purple, he wrote: Turn in homework.

I wrote: Stay home.

"I think you can do better than that," said Daddy.

I wrote: Barf.

Writing that word reminded me that barfing kids get out of all kinds of stuff. All of a sudden, I had a solution.

I wrote: Never mind. I'm fine now.

"Huh?" he asked.

"I have to write something now. Don't peek," I said.

"Never," he said. He made a blindfold out of his bathrobe tie. He stumbled around like he couldn't see. He pretended he stubbed his bare toe. He's a goofy guy sometimes.

He lay down on my bed next to me. He's actually enormous so the whole thing screeched. The mattress sunk. I rolled toward him. I wanted to snuggle him because he was warm and smelled like soap. Only all of that gave me a feeling of guilt because I was about to do something terrible.

"Actually, this is private," I said.

"Oh. In that case, I grant you privacy," he said. "Go to sleep soon, though. It's after midnight!" He kissed my forehead and left.

When I heard his bed creak, I wrote the solution to my problem in my orange pen:

Dear Joan Kleinert,

I am calling you that name on account of I am a grown-up. Lexi cannot do the party. It will make her barf. Please send her to the library until it is over.

Sincerely,

Lexi's dad

I read it a few times. I felt that terrible feeling of guilt get bigger. The naughty list was the pits. This letter was very against the rules. Probably the worst thing I ever did in my whole life.

I tore the letter out of the notebook. I folded it up lots of times. I set it next to the spoon under my pillow to keep it safe.

Guilt still prickled me. Only, I also got to feel relief. My Christmas hoopla problem was finally officially solved and my class could have the party.

I guess that's why I got brave all of a sudden. I decided I wanted to go in the dark. I grabbed my snow day spoon. I thought it could bring good luck. I tiptoed all the way into the dark kitchen. Fred said "Hi" with his squeaks.

"I'm ready to know who's not getting a present tomorrow," I said.

I turned on the sink light because it's not too bright. The floor felt chilly under my bare toes as I walked over to Fred's cage. I got a shiver. Then, I took his food bowl out of his cage. The tiny paper I pulled out of the ski hat was still there. I didn't peek at the name of the kid I was supposed to get a present for yet.

Instead, I squeezed my eyes shut. I held

my spoon extra tight. I wished for a miracle. "I really hope it's someone who doesn't like Christmas hoopla," I said.

Then I opened the paper.

Breaking news.

It said: Kaylee

7

The Party

The next morning, I woke up with the miracle spoon stabbing my cheek. My tummy felt like sour milk.

Without getting out of bed, I peeked out my window. Guess what. No extra snow. No snow day. That's how come I had to dress in extra-warm clothes and stick that awful note in my pocket.

"I did a bad thing," I said at breakfast. I

was trying to eat runny, blucky eggs. They gave me the feeling of barf. "I didn't tell you I have a Present Partner Party today. Can we buy a present at the drugstore?" I asked.

I figured I could give Kaylee the present before I turned in my note.

Mom was busy looking for work shoes under the couch. She stopped for a second and looked at me. "You're usually very good at managing these things, Lexi. Mistakes happen, and I wish I could help. I can't be late for my meeting, though."

I slumped.

"I do have some presents that I bought for you for Christmas. Perhaps you can bring one of those?"

"Well, that's a big, fat relief," I said.

She went to her room for a minute. I stabbed my egg yolks with my fork. They ran into my toast. "At least one problem is solved," I said to myself.

Except, when she came back, I realized I had another problem. She was holding my dream present. A barfing snowman.

"It's the only thing that seemed the right price for a school party," she said. "You could tell your teacher you forgot a gift, or you could give this snowman away."

Both choices were the pits.

I put my chin on the kitchen table. It smelled like egg goop. I thought about Kaylee's face after I didn't turn in my work. I thought about how bad it feels to get on the naughty list. I thought of how breaking rules can destroy people's magic. I am not a fan of any of those things.

I got up and went over to the paper chain by the junk food cupboard. I ripped off that last crummy loop. I took a deep breath like I'm supposed to when I'm not calm. Then I finally said, "Door two."

That's how come I had a snowman gift bag with glitter tissue paper in my hands when I got to school. I could tell the whole day was going to be different the second I got there. Kids were running around the desks even though they still had boots and snow pants on. The flash card table had a bunch of grocery bags on it. Also, the construction paper counter was covered in presents.

Kaylee had a big present in her hands. Her wrapping paper was sparkly silver and blue. Kaylee never uses pink, like me. She was very excited about that party. Not like me. I think I was the only kid who wasn't.

"I got Ruhan a box of gel pens," she said. "It even has the sparkly gold one."

"You don't even like him," I said.

"You get who you get, and you don't throw a fit," she said.

I slumped. "Christmas is one giant compromise."

"Who did you get?" she asked.

I hid the bag with both my mittens to keep it a secret. "No peeking," I said.

Christopher yelled, "Hey, Lexi's here!" Everybody stopped. Their eyeballs stared at me. I have a phobia of that, but I got the guts anyway. The guts is when you do the right thing, even though it gives you the feeling of barf.

My boots weighed 197 pounds on my way to my desk. Not a single kid made a peep. My desk creaked when I opened it. I got my seatwork and put it in the Turn-in Bin.

"Party time!" yelled Christopher. Everybody cheered.

Kaylee did the big smile that shows all her missing teeth.

Ms. Kleinert jingled some jingle bells. I guess that's how she gets kids' attention at winter parties. My insides got hard and cold. "OK, students, set your gifts on the present table. Hang up your coats. We have a busy day!"

She wasn't kidding. First, we had a winter word search. Then, we had to act polite while first-graders sang holiday songs at us. Then, we ate latkes. Those are like giant, smashed French fries. Actually, they were quite yummy. Then, we made gingerbread houses out of graham crackers and milk cartons.

Normally on Fridays, we do journals, then

language arts, then snack, then math. The whole day was screwed up. I didn't even know what time it was.

I kept trying to give Ms. Kleinert the note, but she was busy. Also, I was terrified.

Finally, when we normally have social studies, it was time for Present Partners. Ms. Kleinert rang her jingle bells. All the kids got squealy and wiggly except for me. My insides got hard like an ice cube. My tummy hurt. Mornings are not for junk food, and I ate a whole bunch of gingerbread house supplies. Also, that latke didn't feel delicious anymore. It felt like a lump.

I thought about the ants I was going to get from Christopher. I thought about the music that was going to blare. I thought about all the kids cheering and squealing and how Ms. Kleinert was not going to take marbles out of the jar. Being loud was not against the rules today.

I thought about that note in my pocket. Showing it to Ms. Kleinert was a terrible choice. Sometimes, none of our choices are good.

That's how come I stood up. I walked over to her. She is a big and squishy lady. I tapped her back, which felt soft and happy like marsh-mallows. I did not want to hurt her feelings by making a bad choice. Only I had to.

She turned around and put her face near mine. "Yes, Lexi?" she asked.

I handed her the note. She opened it. Her face looked serious. I watched her brown eyeballs go side-to-side as she read it. Then, she put her hand on my shoulder. Only she didn't look at me. She looked at every-body else and said, "Class, please turn your word searches over. Draw pictures of winter activities on the backs for a few minutes."

Then, she turned my body around. She led me into the hall. The hall is where kids go when they are in big, fat trouble. I never had to go out there for that reason before. Sometimes when I have a bathroom pass, I like how quiet it is out there. Only, it didn't even feel like the same place. Lots of parties were happening in the classrooms out there. It felt like everybody in the whole world was having fun except for me. My eyeballs felt hot and burny.

Ms. Kleinert leaned over and looked at me very serious. "Lexi, your dad didn't write this note."

I looked at the carpet. I couldn't even tell that it was actually a bunch of different colors of brown. It looked like a big, blobby blur. A tear rolled down my nose.

"Lexi, please look at me."

I looked at her mouth. It was still smiley even when she was getting me in big, fat trouble.

"I think this letter is from you," she said.

Lots of tears fell out at that.

"Why don't you want to go to the party, Lexi?" she asked.

I shrugged my shoulders and wiped my face with my sweater.

She waited.

For some reason, that made cry-noises fall out too. Finally, I figured out she wasn't going to budge until I said my answer.

"Hoopla," I said. My voice was a teensy squeak.

Ms. Kleinert is a little bit like my grandma. She has wrinkly skin and she doesn't yell even when you're in big, fat trouble. "Well, I think you propose a good solution, Lexi. The library might be just the place for you to relax a bit. I'd like you to go there if you feel you need a break. You can come back when you're ready."

"Is this big, fat trouble?" I asked.

"No. Of course, it's wrong to lie. I hope you won't do that again. But, not every part of school is right for every kid. Some kids can't do PE. Some kids do different math or reading work. Some kids can't have school lunches. Some kids are better off without class parties. There's no reason to be shy about it."

"So this is a compromise?" I asked.

"Yes," she said.

Breaking news. I did not slump!

I guess compromises aren't when you agree to do something you don't actually like. Maybe compromises are when you get to do a little of what you do like.

"So if I'm not in trouble, can I bring my bunny book to the library?" I asked.

"Sure. Just give me a minute." She went in the classroom. She had me wait outside. That way, the class didn't see my face filled with snots and tears. I wiped it dry the best I could. I could hear Hanukkah music in one of the rooms. Lots of voices sounded happy and loud. I felt tiny in that big hallway.

When Ms. Kleinert came back, I noticed she smelled like laundry soap. She had a tissue, my book, a box of markers, and a piece of blank paper. "Just in case you need something else to do," she said.

She let me walk to the library all by myself. Ms. Alcrey the librarian was expecting me. She let me sit in the yellow beanbag. The air smelled like books. The lights in the library did not buzz. It felt like the kind of place bunnies would enjoy.

I got to read my bunny book. Only this time, I looked at the pictures, not the words. My favorite was of Diego, the kid bunny. He was sitting in front of the Christmas tree. The room was dark except for the lights from the tree. Also, there was a fire in the fireplace. It didn't even look terrifying. Diego was like an elf, making presents in that picture. He looked peaceful. That's how come I felt peaceful.

When I got that feeling, I wanted to use the paper. On one side, I wrote all the things I liked about the party: word search, keeping a Christmas secret from Kaylee, my gift bag, latkes, bringing a barfing snowman for Kaylee, gingerbread house supplies. On the other side, I wrote the things I didn't like: hoopla, squealy kids, singing kids, not seeing Kaylee open her present, getting ants.

Then I drew circles around my lists. Guess what? The circle of things I liked was bigger than the circle of things I didn't.

When the big hand of the clock was on the eleven, I decided to go back to the party. I figured I could survive five minutes. When I walked in, Kaylee smiled at me with all her missing teeth. The sparkly snowman bag was on her desk.

The kids were squealy and wiggly. Wrapping paper was all over the place. Lots of people were playing with new toys. Ruhan, Christopher, and Phoebe were even crawling around on the floor.

I guess it was free time. That's how come Kaylee did not get in trouble when she yelled, "Lexi! I waited for you to open it!" Then she took the tissue paper out of the bag. When she saw what was inside, she squealed. "A barfing snowman!"

She got so happy about that thing that she tap-danced. For the first time ever, I was almost a fan of hoopla.

8

The Christmas Surprise

Even though I was officially on the naughty list, I felt cheery that night after dinner. The house felt cozy. Like a bunny cave. Fred was running around in his big indigo ball in the living room. All the lights were off except for the Christmas tree. Outside the window, the lights on the bushes glowed under the snow. It looked quite beautiful. My mom and daddy were busy baking pies for the big day. The house smelled like cinnamon. I liked that smell.

"This cozy place gives me an idea," I yelled.

"What idea, Lexi?" asked my mom from the kitchen.

"I'd like hot chocolate. Also, I would like a fire."

My mom came into the living room. She wiped her hands on her pants. They were white with flour, the way Ms. Kleinert's pants get white from chalk. "Did you say you'd like a fire?"

"A cozy one."

"Will it make you feel unsafe?" she asked.

"Does glass catch on fire?" I asked.

"No."

"Then maybe you could shut the fireplace doors. So it's not scary."

"I'll get the matches," said Mom. "And hot cocoa. Marshmallows?"

"Duh," I said.

She laughed at that.

"Also, I need some privacy," I said. "I have some Christmas surprises."

"Tonight's a big night for you," she said. "You haven't liked surprises or fires in the past."

I thought about Kaylee's happy dance. She danced even more when I told her she could have whatever Christopher got me. When she found out that gross present was a giant, furry, fake spider, she did a cartwheel.

My insides felt like hot chocolate just thinking about that. "I'm not very good at getting surprises," I said. "But I think giving them might be one of my superpowers."

While my mom got matches and hot chocolate, I looked for supplies. I got construction paper, scissors, a pair of Daddy's socks, cotton balls, and glue. I put those things in a pile on the floor. I threw a blanket over them so my mom couldn't peek.

She lit the fire. She gave me cocoa with foamy, melty marshmallows. She shoved some parsley in Fred's exercise ball. Daddy clanged around in the kitchen. All of those things made me feel cozy inside.

After Mom gave me privacy, I got to work. I glued cotton balls all over the socks for new slippers for Daddy. I made the longest paper chain on Planet Earth for some Christmas tree garland for my mom. Then I made a tiny paper chain using folds instead of glue for Fred. I felt like an elf, or like Diego the bunny from my book.

I worked and worked until I finished all those things. The fireplace crackled. It didn't even make me terrified. Also, the air smelled like pine needles. My insides filled up with Christmas spirit. Also, they felt relaxed from hot cocoa.

"When you think about it, Christmas can actually be quite cozy," I yelled toward the kitchen.

"The quiet moments are my favorite part of Christmas," said Mom.

I gathered those presents up. I hid them in a very secret spot in the hall closet so I could wrap them later. I felt like an elf. "I always thought Christmas equaled hoopla," I said.

"Just a part, not all," said Mom. She was doing dishes now on account of she was done with her projects, too. Daddy banged around putting stuff away.

"I guess the quiet stuff is my favorite part of Christmas, too," I said.

While I was doing spec check for paper

chain pieces, Daddy came in with a kitchen towel hanging over his eyes. He had a present in his hand. "I'm not peeking," he said. "I was just cleaning out your backpack and found this." He held the present out in the wrong direction on account of he could not see me. That guy is a goof.

"I don't need privacy anymore," I said.

He took the towel off his head. Mom came in. I guess that present made her curious.

"What the heck is this?" I asked. I couldn't see too well because it was so dark. I took the present over by the fireplace. It was wrapped in silver paper with a blue bow. That looked familiar. There was a card with my name on it, only I didn't read it. I read cards last.

I unwrapped the present carefully. I don't rip. That's when I discovered a Christmas miracle.

"A barfing snowman!" I said.

"Who's it from?" asked Mom.

"I don't know," I said. I tore the plastic off the package and opened the door on the snowman's back. That's where you stick the candies in.

Mom grabbed the card because grown-ups like those boring things.

I made the snowman's mouth barf a few times. I wasn't very good at first, but after I practiced, the candy shot out and hit my dad's bare feet. It felt good to know that the slippers I made would keep his feet warm soon.

"Lexi, take a look at this," said Mom. She handed me the card. On the front was a picture of two elf-friends, hugging. On the inside, this is what it said:

Dear Lexi,
You're not on my naughty list! Merry Christmas.
Your best friend,
Kaylee

Kaylee must have snuck that thing in my backpack while I was at the library. An explosion of happiness made giggles come

out of me. "Maybe I'm not on the naughty list anymore," I said.

"Lexi, you were never on the naughty list," said my mom. That was actually breaking news. All of a sudden, my insides felt like hot chocolate.

"That is a surprise," I said.

"You don't like surprises," said Daddy. He stole my snowman and pretended to eat the

92

candy. I jumped on him and tickled his arm-pits until he dropped it. Then Mom tickled mine! Then Fred came up in his indigo ball and bonked against us. He wanted to play, too.

I grabbed my snowman back. "I like this surprise," I said. Inside my head, my "like it" circle got even bigger. "I guess I am a fan of Christmas after all!"

Check out

www.EmmaLesko.com

for Lexi's:

- Word Games
- Gross-Out Pranks
- Video Games
- Contests
- Kid Recipes
- Free Stuff

Don't miss Lexi's first book:

SUPER LEXI

Emma Lesko

grew up near Detroit, Michigan, where she ate dirt, taught her guinea pig to turn the basement lights on with his teeth, and read books in a garbage can. Like all kids, Emma had some superpowers. She had supersonic ears, super-strong taste buds, and a super-smelling nose. Sometimes her superpowers were spectacular, and sometimes they gave her a feeling of barf. Though Emma has written a gazillion kids' stories, this is the first series she ever showed anybody.

Adam Winsor

grew up near Raleigh, North Carolina, where he explored the forest, drew comic books, and collected dead bugs from those filter holes in the sides of the swimming pool. He despised music class, hated eyeballs staring at him, and in the middle of one performance, wrapped himself entirely in the American flag he was holding so that no one would see his face. He has worked on several illustration and animation projects for kids, but this is the first chapter book series.

CPSIA information can be obtained
at www.ICGtesting.com
Printed in the USA
LVOW01s2332260416
485475LV00013B/201/P